ARTSY ALPHABET

Written and Illustrated by

Dr. Kimberly Brayman

For information regarding permission please write to:

Dr. Kimberly Brayman: info@KimberlyBraymanAuthor.com

For bulk and wholesale orders please email Dr. Kimberly Brayman: info@KimberlyBraymanAuthor.com

ISBN: 978-1-951688-04-2 (paperback)

Written and Illustrated by: Dr. Kimberly Brayman

First Edition

Team Published with Artistic Warrior

This book is for
Atreus, Henry, Georgia, Penelope,
Caroline, Jaxon, and Jayce
and for all the little ones
learning their ABCs.

B is for Bighorn, you see from afar.

C is for Car,

all rusty and old.

D is for Dog,

that does
what it's told.

E is for Elephant,

tall, big
and strong.

F is for Fish, gently swimming along.

H is for Horses, who like to eat hay.

I is for Imagine,
a world that is kind.

J is for Joy,
the feeling is mine.

K is
for
Koala,

who lives in a tree.

M is for Magical
stories to tell.

N is for
Night, as we bid
day farewell.

O is for Old things,

we often don't see.

P is for Polar bear, wild and free.

Q is for Quest,

in the sun
and the rain

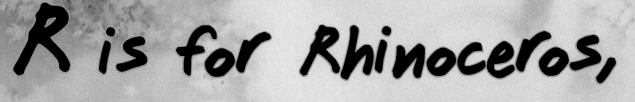

R is for Rhinoceros,

who lives
on the plain.

S is for Sunflower, yellow and bright.

T is for Tortoise, who sleeps in the night.

U is for Unicorn
from a strange land.

V is for Violets,
a bouquet in hand.

W is for witch,
who often
casts
spells.

Y is for Yellow,
a sunflower
bright.

Z is for Zebra, with stripes black and white.

About the Author

Dr. Kimberly Brayman is a licensed psychologist in both Canada and the United States. After decades of working in health care she was inspired to build confidence, normalize struggle, inspire hope, and delight adults and children alike through her storytelling.

She believes stories build empathy and empower the listener to find their own self-reliance and strength. The power of supportive relationships is a strong theme. When a child knows deep in their heart that they are loved and accepted, just the way they are, they have a chance to blossom.

She is a registered psychologist with registration #2464 in British Columbia and licensed psychologist registration #3132 in Colorado.

Dr. Brayman also loves to create with almost anything she can find. In this book she has graced the pages with some of her whimsical water colours.

Illustrated Books by Dr. Kimberly Brayman

Nana Loves You More

Coming Soon!
I am Different and I am the Same
Atreus and the Fisherman
Do I Have To?

Young Readers Chapter Books

Marshmallow the Magic Cat Adventures

Avry's Magical Cat: A Marshmallow the Magic Cat Adventure.
Avry adopts a magical cat from the animal shelter and discovers he is magical like her Nana. She lives close to nature and has a magical view of the world. ***Now Available!***

Avry and Atreus Save Christmas: A Marshmallow the Magic Cat Adventure.
A delightful Christmas tale to be read every holiday season. It's full of elves, ravens, and the capability inside all children to redeem themselves and be good. Available Christmas 2020.

A Troll in the Woods: A Marshmallow the Magic Cat Adventure
A true quest that shows courage and fear can go hand in hand, and the power of friendship to inspire action. Coming Soon.

Marshmallow Paints the Town: A Marshmallow the Magic Cat Adventure
A fun story that focuses on collaboration, self-responsibility, making mistakes and recovering. Coming Soon.

A Trip to the Hot Springs: A Marshmallow the Magic Cat Adventure
A lovely story with a focus on friendship, magic, and skills to assist with anxiety. Coming Soon.

Check the author's website at KimberlyBraymanAuthor.com for updates on when books are available for puchase online.

Made in the USA
Monee, IL
27 October 2021